"RUN DUCK HIDE!"

The Martians Are Coming?

MARION CARLSON

Illustrations by Joshua Allen

AuthorHouse™ LLC
1663 Liberty Drive
Bloomington, IN 47403
www.authorhouse.com
Phone: 1-800-839-8640

© 2014 Marion Carlson. All Rights Reserved.

No part of this book may be reproduced, stored in a retrieval system,
or transmitted by any means without the written permission of the author.

Published by AuthorHouse 05/08/2014

ISBN: 978-1-4969-1042-4 (sc)
ISBN: 978-1-4969-1041-7 (e)

Library of Congress Control Number: 2014908264

Any people depicted in stock imagery provided by Thinkstock are models,
and such images are being used for illustrative purposes only.
Certain stock imagery © Thinkstock.

This book is printed on acid-free paper.

Because of the dynamic nature of the Internet, any web addresses or links contained in this book may have changed since publication and may no longer be valid. The views expressed in this work are solely those of the author and do not necessarily reflect the views of the publisher, and the publisher hereby disclaims any responsibility for them.

Dedication:

To my children, grandchildren and great- grandchildren,
also in memory of my late husband.

"Run --duck–hide!"

The Martians Are Coming?

It was a warm, sunny summer day when Nick decided to leave his weeding job in his aunt's garden to go for a walk in the nearby meadow. He called to her dog, Benna, who quickly came running and followed him.

He and the dog had only been sitting in the shade of the lofty elm tree for a few minutes when suddenly Nick's heart started pounding inside his chest, as he heard a strange sounding voice say, "Run, duck, hide! The Martians are coming!"

Oh, how he wanted to do just that, but his feet wouldn't move!

He couldn't run, duck or hide! Somehow his curiosity was piqued. He wanted to see if this really was a spaceship with Martians, if and where it would land, not to mention that he certainly would like to see what was inside of it.

What was happening?   Was he dreaming?   Who could he tell?

Finally he got his feet moving and quickly stepped up behind the big old elm tree where just a few minutes earlier he had been sitting in its shade enjoying the warm summer day with Benna. Now Nick was peering at the spaceship floating and tipping gracefully in giant circles as it approached the big field in front of him for an apparent landing.

The flashing lights and the brightness of the machine coming nearer to Nick made him hug the tree harder because the closeness and apparent landing was blinding him. He covered his glasses with his hands but kept peeking through his partly open fingers so as not to miss a bit of the action.

Pressing his body even tighter against the tree trunk, Nick watched as this big blob of light and noise circled right over him brushing the top of the elm tree as it made its way to the center of the grassy field. It seemed to be dropping straight down from its place in the sky to the waiting ground. Oh, how he wished someone was here to share this scary, strange, but wonderful experience with him!

Everything inside of Nick was pounding and burning. Now the beeping noise of the approaching space vehicle deafened him. His hands quickly flew from his eyes, which he now tried to hold tightly shut, to his ringing ears. Once again he should run and escape this torture to his body but his feet were glued to the spot and the desire to see more and find out everything he could about was going on held him captive.

Suddenly all was silent! It was as silent as it had been noisy. Once again Nick squinted his tightly shut eyes straining to see through his now smudged glasses, while reaching his head around the tree somewhat so as to see just what was going to happen next.

All he could hear now was the thumping and bumping of his being, so he took some *d-e-e-p* breaths, hoping all the while that they could not hear what seemed to him like awfully loud noises that were going on inside of him, because now the landing scene became deadening silence after all the noise and commotion of before.

Within a few seconds, which seemed like many minutes, the lights began flashing again. This time they were like a huge searchlight whirling around in a circle seeking out something, anything! Round and round went this beam of bright green-colored light. It looked as if the middle of the spaceship where the windows had been was now only a circle of yellow light. The brightness made it very hard to see so Nick quickly covered his eyes with his hands again, all the time peeking through his partly open fingers, and using them with the smudged glasses as filters against this glaring scene, He still did not want to miss anything!

Everything inside of Nick was at attention as he waited, motionless, still using the tree to hide behind so as not to be seen!

What was going to happen?

Suddenly, this green glare of circling light stopped and the silence became oh so heavy once more. Nick wanted to run, but again, could not for the forces inside him held sway over his thinking so certainly over his ability to move.

Now again he squeezed the tree trunk harder and continued to peer gently around it hoping to see everything that was happening.

The bright yellow windows had now become a door from which came a great, shining staircase. A beam of that same bright-colored light shone through the door opening and down the stairs. Behind the beam of light came a little blob of green and orange that looked like a miniature version of the spaceship, having short, fat legs instead of wheels. It had a pear-shaped body with a band of glittering orange light tied around its middle. Its head seemed to be like a bag tipped upside down and made of the same glittering orange light, carrying two shiny silver antennas. It was all so very bright that Nick could hardly look at it, so he could not tell if it had eyes or ears or a nose or mouth or anything for that matter. It just appeared as an intense light bobbing up and down.

Squinting harder, with his body still pressed firmly against the tree trunk, Nick strained as he hoped to see more of what was inside this mechanical wonder. The brightness and continued movement hindered his quest, but he managed to distinguish five such creatures, which by now he had decided were really, truly *Martians* coming down off the stairs!

They each carried one of those same piercing green lights, somewhat like a flashlight only longer and thinner with a much brighter beam. These five "blobs" flashed their lights here and there and all over. Each of them went slowly, carefully, in a different direction always shining their light all around before moving cautiously forward.

Then it happened! One of those lights shone right into his face. It made Nick feel hot all over! Quickly, he pulled himself inside, sliding down the trunk, crouching on the ground .putting his hands over his head, not daring to open his eyes the least little bit. He stayed there trembling, listening, wondering what was to come. His thoughts ran wild, "What would these Martians do with me, where would they take me and what about the dog?"

Suddenly, Benna's loud *yap, yap*, filled the air. Nick jumped to his feet in great surprise without even thinking about anything that was or had been going on!

Green-colored lights flashed every which way. Shrieking and beeping sounds could be heard in every inch of the air. The green and orange blobs of light bobbed here, there, and all over as they scampered pell-mell back to the stairs. It seemed as if they were bumping into and falling over each other in their haste. Then, in a moment, the staircase disappeared, signaling the bright green circle of light to reappear just as before like a huge searchlight flashing rapidly in a large circle.

The steady *yap, yap* barking of the dog could be heard off and on breaking through the noise of the Martian ship. Here stood Nick still next to the tree, speechless and wide-eyed, watching all that was happening so quickly.

Now the spaceship was quiet momentarily, the bright yellow windows having replaced the large door. The beeping sounds rang out loud and clear so Nick's hands flew to cover his ringing ears as the frantic machine began to tilt and list as it rose almost as straight up as it had earlier come down, only faster now so as to escape the fierce, barking animal.

The bright, blinking lights faded while the noise lessened so Nick, with Benna following, ran quickly to the spot in the center of the big field where it had been. The earth felt warm beneath his feet as he raised his arms in wild, waving motions while calling loudly, "Come back, Martians, come back. Don't leave. Let me see you and your machine and how you operate!"

Nick was still sitting under the lofty elm when he realized Benna was slobbering him with her hot, wet tongue while her front paws rested on his shoulders.

Nick and the dog walked, this time for real, to the center of the big field.

Standing there with Benna by his side, Nick began to feel very foolish!

What had he really seen? What had he really heard and what made the dog suddenly start to bark? Who would ever believe him? Had he been dreaming?

Had the Martians really come?

The end

CPSIA information can be obtained at www.ICGtesting.com
Printed in the USA
BVOW10s2036270514

354665BV00002B/2/P